Elliot
Digs for Treasure

For Lucy, Tom and Ellen

Elliot Moose

Elliot Moose™ Andrea Beck Inc.
Text and illustrations © 2001 Andrea Beck Inc.

Kids Can Press acknowledges the financial support of the Ontario Arts Council, the Canada Council for the Arts and the Government of Canada, through the BPIDP, for our publishing activity.

Published in Canada by
Kids Can Press Ltd.
29 Birch Avenue
Toronto, ON M4V 1E2

Published in the U.S. by
Kids Can Press Ltd.
2250 Military Road
Tonawanda, NY 14150

The artwork in this book was rendered in pencil crayon. The text is set in Minion.

Edited by Debbie Rogosin
Designed by Karen Powers
Printed in Hong Kong by Book Art Inc., Toronto

This book is smyth sewn casebound.

CM 01 0 9 8 7 6 5 4 3 2 1

Canadian Cataloguing in Publication Data

Beck, Andrea, 1956–
   Elliot digs for treasure

"An Elliot Moose story."
ISBN 1-55074-806-8

I. Title.

PS8553.E2948.E343 2001   jC813'.54   C00-932859-9
PZ7.B42E1 2001

Kids Can Press is a Nelvana company

Elliot
DIGS FOR TREASURE

Written and Illustrated by
ANDREA BECK

KIDS CAN PRESS

ELLIOT MOOSE was digging a hole.
He'd started right after lunch and by the time his
friend Socks came along, he was almost up to his knees.

"What are you doing?" asked Socks.

"I'm digging for treasure!" said Elliot.

"Treasure?" cried Socks.
"I'll help!"

She grabbed a shovel and hopped into the hole.

By the time Beaverton came along, they were almost up to their middles. He found a shovel and began to dig, too.

Before long, they were all the way up to their shoulders.

By the time Angel arrived, it was getting hard to throw the dirt out of the hole. When they told her about the treasure, she wanted to help, too.

"I'll take the dirt away!" she said.

Soon, all that could be seen were the tips of Elliot's ears.

The friends dug deeper and deeper.

"We must be getting close to the treasure now!"
said Elliot. And just then, his shovel hit something hard.

Everyone stopped to look.

"Oh, I hope it's a box of jewels!" said Socks.

"Or a chest of coins!" said Beaverton.

But it was only a big rock, so they went right
back to digging.

By now the hole was very deep. Still the friends kept working.

Each time someone hit something hard, they all held their breath. They found a coin, a tin whistle and an old toy truck. But no treasure.

"My arms are tired," said Socks.

"Mine, too," said Beaverton.

So they all flopped down for a little rest.

Angel peered in from above.

"Did you find the treasure?" she called eagerly.

In her excitement, she leaned too far and fell tip over tail into the hole!

"This hole is *very* deep," she said as she dusted herself off. "Are you sure there's really a treasure here?"

"Of course!" said Elliot proudly. "I found this map. See the big X? An X always means treasure."

Angel stared at the paper.

"Elliot," she cried. "That's Lionel's garden map! The X is where he's planting his tree."

"His tree?" said Elliot.

Then he remembered the little seedling that Lionel had been tending for weeks.

Elliot looked sadly at his friends. "I'm sorry," he said. "I really thought there was a treasure here."

"Well," said Beaverton, "at least we've helped Lionel. But we've dug an *awfully* big hole for that teeny tiny tree!"

Then he winked at Elliot and began to chuckle.

Soon, everyone was laughing — even Elliot.

Elliot felt a little silly, but he
didn't *really* mind about the treasure.
He loved to dig, and today they'd
dug the biggest, deepest hole ever.
They'd found some interesting
things — and they'd helped Lionel.

Now it was time for supper.

Elliot looked up.

Uh-oh! They'd forgotten
something.

The others looked up, too.
"Oh dear," said Beaverton.
"How are we going to get out?" cried Socks.
They were trapped in the hole!

After a few worried minutes, they came up with a plan. Beaverton knelt down and Elliot got up on his shoulders. Next, Socks scrambled onto Elliot. But even when she stretched, she couldn't quite reach the top of the hole. When Angel clambered up, the fuzzy tower began to sway. Elliot wibbled, Beaverton wobbled and they all came tumbling down.

"Let's call for help," suggested Socks.

The friends began to shout. They yelled and hollered as loud as they could.

But nobody came.

"We need a ladder," moaned Angel.

Elliot sighed. "All we've got is three shovels."

Beaverton began to smile.

"You mean three shovels and a *rock*!" he said.

Everyone watched as Beaverton balanced a shovel on top of the rock.

He asked Angel to stand on one end. Then he told Elliot to climb onto Socks's shoulders.

"Now what?" asked Elliot.

"It's quite scientific really," said Beaverton. "Jump down onto the other end of the shovel."

Elliot took a deep breath and jumped.

"WHEEE!" yelled Angel as she shot up and out of the hole. "I'm flying!"

She ran off, and a few minutes later came back with Lionel. Together, they hoisted Socks, then Beaverton, out of the hole.

At last, it was Elliot's turn. He held on tight as his friends pulled him up, up, up to freedom.

Everyone gathered around while Elliot told Lionel about the map and digging for treasure. Then they showed Lionel the things they'd found.

"A rock with golden sparkles," he marveled. "An ancient coin. A rare tin whistle. And a splendid toy truck. Why, these are magnificent treasures!"

Elliot took a closer look at his truck and smiled.

Angel, Socks and Beaverton were smiling, too.

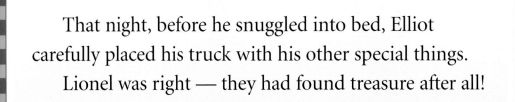

That night, before he snuggled into bed, Elliot
carefully placed his truck with his other special things.
Lionel was right — they had found treasure after all!